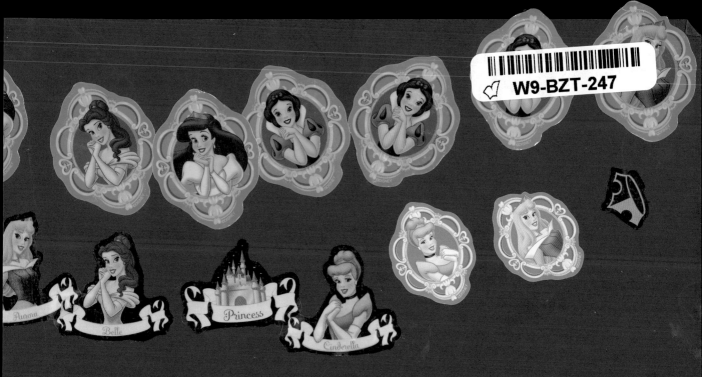

DISNEY's

MICKEY's CHRISTMAS·CAROL

Based on *A Christmas Carol* by
Charles Dickens

Princess

Adapted from the film by
JIM RAZZI

Illustrated by
PHIL WILSON

DISNEY PRESS
NEW YORK

Library of Congress Catalog Card Number: 91-58970
ISBN: 1-56282-238-1 / 1-56282-236-5 (lib. bdg.)

t was a snowy Christmas Eve in old London-town. As the snowflakes drifted gently down onto the gabled roofs and cobblestone streets, Ebenezer Scrooge, the richest, meanest, and stingiest man in town, gripped his cane and picked his way along a bustling thoroughfare.

He trudged by a jolly Santa, who was ringing his bell, urging people to give a shilling or two for the poor. Santa called out, "Merry Christmas!" but the cranky old miser just huddled deeper into his topcoat.

A trio of young lads singing Christmas carols under a lamp-post nodded and smiled as Scrooge passed by. Their pink little faces glowed with good cheer. But Scrooge barely gave them a glance. He only wrapped his wool muffler tighter around his scrawny neck.

"Bah, humbug," he muttered as the carolers' joyous voices followed him down the winding street.

"Singing for Christmas!" he grumbled to himself. "They should be singing for their supper. At least there would be some profit in it."

1

A shivering beggar held out his hand and cried, "Give a penny for the poor, governor."

"Bah," answered Scrooge, waggling his cane at the poor wretch to keep his distance.

Scrooge continued to weave his way through the busy, snow-swept streets. Finally reaching his countinghouse, he let out a deep sigh, as if he had reached a haven of sanity in the midst of all the merry madness.

Scrooge glanced up at the sign that hung above the door. The wooden board was half-covered with snow, but the name *Marley* could be seen crossed out. Jacob Marley had once been Scrooge's partner.

Scrooge gazed wistfully at Marley's name. "Dead seven years today," he said aloud. "Aye, he was a good one." Scrooge chuckled slyly before adding, "He robbed from the widows and swindled the poor. And in his will he left me enough to pay for his tombstone."

Still chuckling, the old miser gave the sign a tap with his cane. The snow fell off in powdery chunks to reveal his own name right above Marley's. Scrooge continued gazing at the sign, a small, satisfied smile on his usually dour face.

"Ha! And I had him buried at sea!" he cackled. With a wag of his head, in appreciation of his own shrewdness, Ebenezer Scrooge marched into his countinghouse.

Scrooge entered just as his clerk, Bob Cratchit, was about to throw a small piece of coal into the old iron stove that stood in the middle of the cold, dark room.

When Bob saw Scrooge, he tried to hide the coal behind his back.

"Oh, ha, ha, ha! G-good morning, Mr. Scrooge," he stuttered.

"Cratchit!" Scrooge growled. "What are you doing with that piece of coal?"

The clerk reached for a frozen quill and ink bottle that lay on top of the stove.

"I was, uh, j-just trying to thaw out the ink," he answered.

With one swift movement, Scrooge knocked the coal out of Bob's hand with his cane. The coal went flying through the air and dropped with a *clunk* into an almost empty coal scuttle.

"Bah!" cried Scrooge. "You used a piece last week. Now get on with your work!"

Without another word, Bob scurried up onto his high stool and hunched over his big black ledger book. A moment later he turned his head and looked beseechingly at his employer.

"Speaking of work, Mr. Scrooge," Bob said hesitantly. "Tomorrow is Christmas and I, uh…"

Scrooge, who was just putting his hat and coat on the hat rack, stopped in midmotion and winced as if in pain.

"…I was wondering," Bob continued, "if I could have, uh, half a day off?"

For a long silent moment Scrooge appeared to struggle with a great decision. Finally he sighed and said, "I suppose so." But in the next breath he shook a finger and added, "But I'll dock you half a day's pay."

Bob nodded in eager agreement.

"Now, let's see," Scrooge said thoughtfully. "I pay you two shillings a day…."

"Two shillings and a halfpenny, sir," Bob respectfully reminded him.

"Oh, yes," answered Scrooge. "I gave you that raise three years ago."

"Yes, sir," Bob said, "when I started doing your laundry."

"Hmph," Scrooge said, remembering. Then, with a hard look, he muttered, "All right, Cratchit, get busy while I go over my accounts."

But before he reached his desk, Scrooge walked over to a sack lying on the floor and tossed it to his clerk. "And speaking of laundry," he said, "here's another bundle of shirts for you."

"Yes, sir," Bob replied cheerfully as he caught the sack.

And with another "Hmph," Scrooge finally settled down at his desk and took out his money bags. Suddenly his face took on the glow of someone enjoying a delicious meal as he stacked the money in front of him and slowly started counting.

"Ah, let's see now," he murmured. "Fifty pounds, ten shillings from McDuff. Plus his eighty-percent interest, compounded daily."

Ebenezer Scrooge beamed at the sight of the money before him. Suddenly he hugged the gold coins as if they were his best friends.

"Heh, heh, heh…money, money, money!" he cackled.

Just then the doorbell tinkled and a chipper young man burst into the countinghouse.

"Merry Christmas!" he cried.

Bob smiled and jumped down from his stool. "And a Merry Christmas to you, Master Fred," he said.

Scrooge only peered over the stacks of coins at his nephew and growled, "Bah, humbug!"

But if young Fred heard the remark, he didn't let on. Instead, he held up a fragrant green wreath he had brought with him.

"Merry Christmas, Uncle Scrooge," he said.

"What's so merry about it?" Scrooge retorted.

The old miser got up from his desk and advanced upon his nephew like a schoolmaster lecturing a dim-witted pupil.

"I'll tell you what Christmas is," yelled Scrooge, pointing his finger only inches from Fred's face. "It's just another workday. And any jackanapes who thinks otherwise should be boiled in his own pudding!"

Fred playfully backed away from his uncle, holding the wreath before him like a shield.

Before Scrooge could say another word, Bob chimed in, "But, sir, Christmas is a time for giving and a time to be with one's family."

"I say bah, humbug!"

Bob lowered his eyes, but Fred's enthusiasm would not be dampened. "I don't care—I say Merry Christmas, Merry Christmas!" he cried.

Bob couldn't help clapping his hands in agreement. But a stern look from Scrooge stopped him, and the timid clerk pretended he was only trying to keep his hands warm.

"Hmph!" sniffed Scrooge. Then, turning back to Fred, he said, "And what brings you here, Nephew?"

"I've come to give you this and invite you to Christmas dinner," Fred said, handing the wreath to Scrooge with a flourish.

Scrooge stared at Fred a moment. Then his face took on a delighted expression. For a moment, he truly looked like a dear old uncle. In a kindly voice, he said, "Well, I suppose you're going to have plump goose with chestnut dressing?"

Fred nodded eagerly.

"And will you have plum pudding and lemon sauce?" Scrooge went on.

"Yes! Boy, oh boy!" answered Fred. It seemed he could almost taste the food already.

"And candied fruits with sugar cakes?" Scrooge continued.

Fred nodded excitedly. "Yes, all of that," he said. "Will you come, Uncle Scrooge?"

For a moment, Scrooge held his smile. Then without warning, his face screwed up into its usual mean expression, and he backed Fred up against the door.

"Are you daft?" Scrooge sneered. "You know I can't eat that stuff!"

And with that, he opened the door, plopped the wreath over Fred's head, and pushed him out the door into the cold.

"Take your wreath back!" Scrooge cried. "Now, out, out, out!"

The gust of air from the open doorway scattered Cratchit's papers all over the place. The humble clerk scrambled to put them in order, not knowing what would happen next.

But all Scrooge said was, "Bah, humbug." And he slammed the door shut.

As he started to walk back to his desk, however, the door opened again and Fred poked his head in. With a quick flick of his wrist, he hung the wreath on the inside knob and whisked the door closed once more.

Then, at the top of his lungs, he yelled, "Merry Christmas!"

Scrooge whirled around and yelled back, "And a Bah, humbug to you!"

Bob couldn't help smiling now. "That Fred, always so full of kindness," he said, more to himself than to Scrooge.

"Aye," answered Scrooge with a thoughtful look. "He always *was* a little peculiar."

Scrooge and Bob settled back into their seats. Yet no sooner had they started to work, when the bell over the front door

tinkled again, and two gentlemen entered the room. One was tall and thin. The other was short and round. Both were fashionably dressed.

"Customers," Scrooge murmured, rubbing his hands together.

Bob was about to get up, but Scrooge waved him off.

"I'll handle this, Cratchit," he said.

The two men stood awkwardly, waiting for Scrooge to approach them.

"Hmm, yes, what can I do for you two gentlemen?" asked Scrooge.

The thin man cleared his throat and said in a crisp voice, "Sir, we are soliciting funds for the…ah…hum…for the indigent and destitute."

"For the what?" Scrooge asked impatiently.

"We're collecting money for the poor," the shorter man chimed in.

"Ohhhhh, aha, the poor," Scrooge said, raising an eyebrow. He gazed at the men thoughtfully before continuing. "Well," he finally said, "you do realize that if you give money to the poor, they won't be poor anymore, will they?"

The two men looked at each other and then back at Scrooge. They nodded doubtfully, not quite sure they understood what Scrooge was getting at.

"And if they're not poor anymore," Scrooge went on, "then you won't have to raise money for them anymore, will you?"

"Well, I suppose not…." the thin one said.

"And if you don't have to raise money for them anymore," Scrooge concluded, "then you'll be out of a job, won't you?"

Scrooge spread his hands and put on a pained expression as he backed the solicitors out the door.

"Oh, please, gentlemen, don't ask me to put you out of a job," he said. "Not on *Christmas Eve.*"

"Oh, we wouldn't do that, Mr. Scrooge," the two men earnestly assured him.

"Well then," Scrooge cried, snatching the wreath off the doorknob and throwing it at them, "I suggest you give *this* to the poor and begone!"

The wreath landed right around the nose of the smaller man. Both men stood in total confusion as Scrooge slammed the door in their face.

"What's this world coming to, Cratchit?" Scrooge muttered, turning back into the room. "You work all your life to get money, and people want you to give it away."

Bob realized that Scrooge didn't expect an answer, so he just huddled over his desk and continued working. He remained that way for the rest of the day until, finally, the old clock on the wall chimed seven o'clock. Quitting time!

Bob was about to climb down from his stool when he saw Scrooge looking at his pocket watch.

"Hmm, that clock's two minutes fast," Scrooge announced.

Bob quickly took pen in hand and got back to work.

But Scrooge waved one hand in the air as if he were being the most generous person in the world.

"Well, never mind those two minutes. You may go."

"Oh, thank you, sir! You're so kind," Bob said.

"Never mind that mushy stuff, just go," grumbled Scrooge. "But be here all the earlier the next day!"

"I will, I will, sir! And a Bah, humbug, ha, ha, I mean, a Merry Christmas to you, sir!"

"Bahhh," answered Scrooge.

ater that evening, Scrooge made his way home. The streets were deserted, and the wind whipped the snow through them like a lost and lonely spirit roaming the city. Except for the howling wind, everything was unnaturally quiet. Scrooge shivered and huddled into his topcoat.

When he arrived at his dark and gloomy house, he gazed up at the door knocker. It was a fine lion's head, and Scrooge had seen it countless times before. But as he stared at it tonight, the lion's head began to change into the very image of his dead partner, Jacob Marley. Scrooge couldn't believe his eyes.

"Ehh-beh-nee-zer Scroooge," an unearthly voice broke the silence.

Scrooge gasped and took a step back. The voice was coming from the door knocker—from Marley's head!

"Jacob Marley?" Scrooge whispered fearfully. "No, it can't be!"

With a violent shudder, Scrooge yanked open the front door and dashed into his house.

Once inside, he took a deep breath. But as he hurried up the stairs to his bedroom, he had a strange feeling he was being followed. Scrooge looked behind him once, then twice, but there was no one there.

Suddenly something lifted the hat right off his head. Scrooge whirled around and saw on the wall the big black shadow of a ghost looming over him.

With a screeching yelp, Scrooge grabbed his hat back. Poking his cane at the shadow, he dashed the rest of the way up the stairs as fast as his legs would carry him. He slammed his bedroom door shut and bolted all of the locks.

He leaned against the heavy door and sighed in relief, but a sudden loud knock gave him a jolt. Scrooge dropped his cane and ran to his chair. He scrunched down low, shaking from head to toe as he stared at the door.

For a moment there was silence, then the same unearthly voice moaned low and slow, "Ehh-beh-nee-zer Scrooooge."

Scrooge cowered against the high arm of his chair and pulled his hat down over his head.

"Go away!" he cried out.

But instead of going away, the ghostly image of Marley passed right through the door and into the room. Even though Scrooge didn't dare look, he could hear the rattling sound of chains being dragged across the floor. Scrooge was shaking even harder than before.

Suddenly he heard a terrible crash and, trembling, peeked out from under his hat. There on the floor was a shadowy figure, sprawled flat on its face. The ghost had tripped over Scrooge's cane!

But no sooner had Scrooge seen the ghost than it disappeared.

As Scrooge sat there quivering, too afraid to move, the ghost suddenly popped up behind the arm of the chair.

"Yeow!" screamed Scrooge.

For a moment the ghost just cocked its head and looked puzzled.

"Scrooge, don't you recognize me?" it asked calmly. "I was your partner, Jacob Marley."

Wide-eyed, Scrooge peered at the ghost.

"Marley. It *is* you!" he said in a whisper.

The ghost nodded solemnly.

"Ebenezer, remember when I was alive, I robbed the widows and swindled the poor?"

Scrooge forgot his fright for a moment and cried, "Yes, yes—and all in the same day! Oh, you had class, Jacob," Scrooge continued admiringly. "Ha, ha, ha! Yes!"

A flicker of pride crossed Marley's face, but the ghost quickly changed its expression. "Ah, no! No! I was wrong!" it said sadly. "And so as punishment, I'm forced to carry these heavy chains throughout eternity."

As it said these words, the ghost tossed and rattled the thick chains that bound it hand and foot. Some of the chains fell around Scrooge, encircling him.

"There's no hope," the ghost went on, rattling its chains. "I'm doomed! Doomed!"

Before Scrooge knew what had happened, he was caught up in the chains along with Marley. He almost choked as the ghost began to wave its arms around in despair.

"And the same thing will happen to you, Ebenezer Scrooge!" Marley's ghost warned.

"No, it can't, it mustn't! Help me, Jacob!" Scrooge pleaded.

But the ghost seemed deaf to Scrooge's pleas. "Tonight, you will be visited by three spirits," it declared, holding up two fingers.

Even as Scrooge cowered, he couldn't help thinking that Marley never *had* been able to count correctly.

"Listen to them," Marley's ghost went on. "Do what they say, or your chains will be even heavier than mine!"

Then the ghost turned to leave.

"Farewell, Ebenezer, and remember my words," it said as it passed back through the door.

And then the room was still except for a quaking Scrooge, who was all alone again.

y the time Scrooge was in his nightgown and ready for bed, he had gotten back some of his courage. In fact, he was beginning to think he might simply have imagined the whole ghostly visit. Even so, he peeked under his bed before blowing out the candle.

"Spirits, eh? Humbug!" he muttered as he climbed into bed and drew the bed curtains.

Scrooge was soon fast asleep. The only sound in the room was the rumble of his snoring....

Ding! Ding! Ding! Ding!

Scrooge tossed in his bed at the sound of his clock bell.

Ding! Ding! Ding! Ding! It rang again.

This time Scrooge opened one eye and peered through the bed curtains.

"Wha...what's happening?" he asked, still half-asleep.

"Well, it's about time," a cranky voice answered. "Haven't got all night, you know!"

Scrooge looked at his night table and saw a small cricket standing there, striking the clock bell with its little red umbrella.

"Who are y-you?" asked Scrooge.

"Why, I'm the Ghost of Christmas Past," the cricket answered. And with that, it proudly showed Scrooge a gold badge attesting to that fact.

Still only half-awake, Scrooge looked at the Ghost of Christmas Past doubtfully.

"Ohhh, I thought you'd be taller," he mumbled.

"Hmph!" replied the ghost. "Listen, Scrooge, if men were measured by kindness, you'd be no bigger than a speck of dust."

Scrooge yawned and said, "Hah! Kindness is of little use in this world."

"You didn't always think so," the ghost replied. "C'mon now, Scrooge, it's time to go."

"Then go," said Scrooge as he snuggled back under his blanket. The ghost hopped up onto the bedroom window and, with a tap of its umbrella, opened it wide. A blast of cold air burst into the room.

"Spirit, what are you doing?" Scrooge yelled.

"We're going to visit your past," said the little ghost, pointing out into the night.

Scrooge got out of bed and cautiously approached the window. The night air chilled his bones, but that wasn't the only reason he was shivering.

"I'm not going out there," Scrooge cried. "I'll fall."

"Just hold on," the ghost said, hopping into Scrooge's hand. Scrooge did as he was told.

"Whoop, not *too* tight now," the tiny creature yelped, squirming inside Scrooge's clamped fist.

The cricket unfurled its red umbrella, and suddenly Scrooge

found himself rising off the ground. The next thing Ebenezer Scrooge knew, he and the ghost were flying out into the snowy night.

"Ooh-ah-ah-oh-oh-oh!" Scrooge wailed.

"What's wrong, Scrooge?" asked the ghost. "I thought you enjoyed looking down on the world."

"Where are we going?" Scrooge asked when he caught his breath.

"I already told you," answered the ghost, "back to your past."

The city passed slowly beneath them as they flew high above its snowcapped roofs and winding streets.

Scrooge looked down at the scene in awe, his nightgown flapping in the frosty air. He noticed that the town looked different—as if there were things about it that were only faintly familiar.

Before long, Scrooge found himself floating back to earth, right in front of a gaily lit warehouse. The building was decorated for Christmas, and the joyful sound of music filled the air.

"Spirit, I believe I know this place," said Scrooge.

He ran over to the frosted pane-glass window and peeked in. A Christmas party was taking place inside the warehouse, and Scrooge recognized many of the rosy faces.

"Yes, it's ol' Fezzywig's!" he exclaimed happily. "I couldn't have worked for a kinder man!"

As Scrooge gazed at the scene, tears formed in his eyes. It was all so cozy and familiar. Why, there was Fezzywig himself, perched way up on his high desk, playing a snappy holiday tune on his fiddle.

"All my very dearest friends," Scrooge said in a choked voice.

Then he spied a shy young lad perched on a crate in a corner of the room.

"Why, that's me!" he cried to the ghost.

The tiny ghost nodded beside him.

"Yes, that was before you became a miserable miser, consumed by greed," the ghost answered.

Scrooge shrugged. "Well, nobody's perfect," he said sheepishly. His eyes were quickly drawn to a perky young girl in the center of the room.

"And there…there's lovely Isabel," he sighed.

Scrooge watched in wonder as the girl walked over to his younger self and took him by the hand. He had forgotten how pretty she was.

Isabel led the young Scrooge to the mistletoe.

"My eyes are closed, my lips are puckered, and I'm standing under the mistletoe," she said invitingly.

"You're also standing on my foot," the old Scrooge heard the young Scrooge retort. And he saw a hurt look pass over Isabel's face.

Scrooge felt like kicking his younger self for being such an insensitive clod. But after an awkward moment, Scrooge saw Isabel grab his former self and begin to dance. The young couple grinned in delight as they twirled and whirled to the happy music.

When the dance was over, Isabel leaned toward young Scrooge and planted a big kiss on his cheek. Even through the frosted window, old Scrooge could see the dazed and happy look on the lad's face.

Scrooge sighed and said in a soft voice, "I remember now how much I was in love with her."

"In ten years' time, you learned to love something else much more," said the ghost.

As the ghost said these words, the street and warehouse slowly faded from view. Suddenly Scrooge found himself in another time and place.

"Why—why it's my countinghouse," Scrooge cried out in surprise. "But it looks so new."

Scrooge peered into the dim light and saw a figure hunched over a tall chair. It was yet another version of himself, sitting at his counting desk. This Scrooge, however, was ten years older than the youth at the party. And this Scrooge already had a look of greed on his face as he counted the stacks of money before him.

"Ebenezer," a soft voice spoke from in front of Scrooge's desk.

It was Isabel, standing before Scrooge with her hands outspread.

"Yes?" the young Scrooge said impatiently. "What is it?"

"For years I've had this honeymoon cottage, Ebenezer," she said humbly. "I've been waiting for you to keep your promise to marry me."

Isabel stood up a little straighter.

"Now I must know," she said. "Have you made your decision?"

The younger Scrooge appeared to be thinking about it. After a tense silence, he smacked his fist into his other hand and cried, "I have!"

Isabel leaned forward, an eager glow in her large eyes. But she recoiled when Scrooge shoved a scroll in her face.

"Your last payment on the cottage was an hour late," he said

gruffly. "I'm foreclosing the mortgage!"

For a second, Isabel seemed too stunned to speak. Then she lowered her eyes and began to weep. She remained that way until Scrooge coldly went back to counting his coins. Then, with her head held high, she marched to the door, looked back once, and was gone.

The old Scrooge quickly took a step forward as if to stop her. But just as quickly he realized that these were only ghosts from the past. He could do nothing to change things now.

"You loved your gold more than that precious creature," the Ghost of Christmas Past declared. "And so you lost her forever."

Scrooge shook his head slowly and wiped a tear from his eye.

"Please, spirit. I can no longer bear these memories," he said. "Take me home."

"Remember, Scrooge," the ghost said softly, "you fashioned these memories yourself…yourself…yourself…."

benezer Scrooge closed his eyes in grief as the ghost's fading words echoed over and over in his head. When he opened his eyes again, he was back in his own bed!

The Ghost of Christmas Past was nowhere to be seen, but the memory of its visit still lingered in Scrooge's mind. The old miser lowered his head as he realized what a fool he had been. He had spent his whole life solely in the pursuit of money.

All of a sudden, a beam of light fell across his face. Scrooge blinked, crawled over to the edge of the bed, and peeked out from the drawn curtain. There, sitting right in the middle of the room, was the biggest ghost he could ever imagine. He couldn't help but notice that this ghost was *so* enormous it couldn't even stand up in the room!

Scrooge held on to the bed curtains with trembling hands as the ghostly giant peered down on him.

"Fee, fi, fo, fum," said the ghost. "I smell a stingy little Englishmun!"

With no more warning than that, the ghost scooped Scrooge up in its huge hand and studied him as if he were some sort of interesting bug.

"Please let me go," Scrooge pleaded. "Don't eat me!"

The ghost shook its head from side to side.

"Why would the Ghost of Christmas Present—that's me—want to eat a distasteful little miser like you?" it answered.

And, holding Scrooge up by the scruff of his neck, the giant gestured at the wonderful feast surrounding them. "Especially when there are so many good things to enjoy in life," it added. "See?"

Scrooge gaped at the abundance of food spread before him. There were candied fruits, a roast suckling pig, and turkey, not to mention mince pies, plum pudding, and so many other tasty things that Scrooge's mouth began to water.

"But where did all this come from?" Scrooge asked.

"From the heart," the ghost replied. "It's the food of generosity, which you have long denied your fellow man."

Scrooge angrily swatted aside a lush bunch of juicy red grapes.

"Generosity, hah!" he cried. "Nobody has ever shown *me* any generosity."

"You've never given them reason to," the ghost pointed out, as it deposited Scrooge in its huge coat pocket. And yet, there are some who still find enough warmth in their hearts even for the likes of you."

"Hah, no acquaintance of mine, I assure you," Scrooge said.

The ghost nodded at Scrooge while it casually pried off the roof of Scrooge's house with one huge hand. "You'll see," it said.

And with that, the ghost stepped over the wall of the house and into the night. It stopped to pluck up a streetlamp, and using that to light the way, the ghost tramped through the

streets with Scrooge safely nestled in its pocket. Scrooge could feel the ground tremble beneath them as they made their way through the silent city.

He peeked out of the giant's pocket, but the blowing snow stung his face, so he huddled back down to keep warm. A few moments later the giant stopped at a small run-down house. A faint but cheery glow could be seen through the window.

The ghost took Scrooge out of its pocket and deposited him in front of the window.

"Why did you bring me to this old shack?" Scrooge asked, shivering.

"This is the home of your overworked, underpaid employee, Bob Cratchit," the giant answered.

Scrooge peered curiously through the window just in time to see Mrs. Cratchit bring a small tin platter to the table. On it was the scrawniest little bird Scrooge had ever seen.

Scrooge raised his eyebrows.

"What's she cooking—a canary?" he sneered. "Surely they have more food than that." And turning his gaze toward a huge iron pot bubbling on the fire, he smiled and nodded.

"Look there, on the fire," he urged the ghost.

"That's your laundry!" the ghost told him.

Scrooge lowered his eyes in sudden shame. But he quickly raised them again when Mrs. Cratchit set the platter on the table and her children burst upon the scene, squealing in delight. They had been decorating a scrawny little Christmas tree in the corner. Although the meager tree sagged under the weight of the pitifully few popcorn balls hung on its fragile branches, the youngsters seemed quite delighted by it.

"Not yet, children," Bob said kindly. "We must wait for Tiny Tim."

Just then Scrooge heard a weak voice call out, "Coming, Father. I'm coming." He turned to see a small boy hobbling down the stairs on a crutch.

Bob lovingly picked up the boy and set him down at the table.

"Oh, my," said Tiny Tim. "Look at all the wonderful things to eat! We must thank Mr. Scrooge."

Scrooge saw the sad look that passed between Bob and his wife as they gazed at the smiling little boy.

"What's wrong with the little lad?" asked Scrooge.

"Much, I'm afraid," answered the ghost, gazing off into the distance. "If these conditions remain unchanged, I see an empty chair where Tiny Tim now sits."

Scrooge's eyes widened.

"Then that means Tim will…"

At that moment, the lights went out, and Cratchit's house became dark and deserted.

Scrooge whirled to face the ghost. But it, too, was gone. There was nothing but a giant footprint in the snow to prove that it had ever been there.

"h-where did everyone go?" Scrooge cried. He turned this way and that, suddenly afraid of being alone in the cold, dark night.

"Spirit, answer me. Don't go," Scrooge pleaded. "You must tell me what will happen to Tim."

But the ghost had disappeared for good. In its place a great fog rolled in, leaving Scrooge to grope blindly through the night.

It was not until a coughing fit overwhelmed him that Scrooge realized it wasn't a fog at all, but great billows of smoke. And as the smoke began to thin out, he saw he was now in a lonely graveyard, leaning against a tombstone for support.

Through the wisps of smoke that remained, he saw an enormous hooded figure, its face shrouded in darkness.

"Oh, wh-where did…? Oh, who are y-you?" Scrooge asked in a trembling voice.

The figure was unmoving and silent.

Then Scrooge understood.

"Are you the Ghost of Christmas Future?" Scrooge asked.

The terrifying figure remained silent, but Scrooge thought he saw it nod.

"Please speak to me," Scrooge pleaded. "Tell me what will happen to Tiny Tim."

In answer, the ghost only turned its hooded face toward a nearby grave and pointed. Scrooge followed the ghostly gaze and saw Bob Cratchit holding Tiny Tim's crutch in his hand, wiping tears from his eyes. Then the grieving clerk gently placed Tim's crutch against the small gravestone and, shoulders stooped, trudged away.

"Oh no," moaned Scrooge. "Spirit, I didn't want this to happen," he said. "Tell me these events can yet be changed."

Scrooge had barely finished his plea when the sound of cackling laughter drifted over to him. It was coming from two gravediggers who were shoveling dirt into an open grave. The grave site was located at a particularly lonely spot in the cemetery.

Scrooge felt himself being drawn toward the spot as if some hidden force was at work. And as he neared the grave site, he could hear the gravediggers' conversation.

"I've never seen a funeral like this," said one.

"Aye, no mourners, no friends to bid him farewell," said the other man.

"Ah, well, let's rest a minute afore we fill it in, hey?" the first gravedigger suggested. "He ain't going nowheres."

His companion agreed with a chuckle, and the two gravediggers laughed uproariously as they walked away from the waiting hole in the ground.

As soon as they were gone, Scrooge found himself standing by the open grave, looking down in fear and dread.

"Spirit, whose lonely grave is this?" he asked.

The still-silent ghost suddenly struck a match on the tomb-

stone, and the flash of light revealed its terrifying face.

"Why, yours, Ebenezer Scrooge," the ghost finally said in a deep voice. "The richest man in the cemetery!" Then it laughed long and loud, and the sound chilled Scrooge to the bone.

Scrooge's eyes opened wide at the sight of his own name carved on the gravestone. The ghost laughed again, and the sound of it made Scrooge cringe.

Teetering at the brink of the hole, Scrooge could see his own coffin below. As he looked down upon it, he suddenly grew dizzy. He clutched at some twisted roots at the edge of the grave to keep from falling.

"Spirit, no," cried Scrooge. "I'll, uh, I'll change my ways!"

But the ghost didn't answer.

Before Scrooge's terrified eyes, a cloud of red smoke billowed up from the coffin, and he suddenly felt as if an invisible hand was forcing him into the deep, dark hole.

"No! No! No...," Scrooge cried over and over while he clung to the roots at the edge of the grave. He looked to the Ghost of Christmas Future for some ray of hope, but the ghost only laughed. Then it disappeared into the fiery red smoke.

Scrooge desperately held on to the roots, but suddenly they tore away from the ground, and Scrooge found himself falling slowly into the deep grave.

The lid of the coffin opened, and huge flames flickered upward like fiery red snakes. "Noooo!" Scrooge cried as he continued to fall. "I'll change! I promise!"

But still he fell, and the open coffin yawned nearer, beckoning to him.

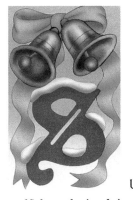

uddenly, without warning, Scrooge found himself back in his own bed again.

"Why, I'm home, in my own room," he said aloud, letting out a long sigh.

It was then that he heard the church bells ringing, and he laughed to himself.

"It's Christmas morning!" he exclaimed gleefully.

Ebenezer Scrooge ran to the window and threw it open to the frosty morning air. But now he didn't mind the cold at all.

"I haven't missed it," he cried out to the city at large. "The spirits have given me another chance!"

As if in agreement, a flock of snow-white doves flew up from the windowsill and soared into the clear blue sky.

Scrooge ran around the room in a frenzy of joy. "I know just what I'll do!" he cried in delight. "They'll be so surprised!"

He rubbed his hands together and said, "Oh, what a wonderful day, ha, ha, ha, hee!"

Scrooge was in too much of a hurry to dress himself properly. He pulled his topcoat on over his nightgown and set his hat upon his head.

"There's so much to do, so much to do! Hee, hee," he chortled as he headed for the door.

In a twinkling, he was bouncing merrily down the stairs. But suddenly he stopped and looked down at himself. Then he ran back up the stairs and dashed into his bedroom.

"I can't go out like *this*!" he said.

He rummaged through his things until he found what he wanted.

"There, that's better," Scrooge said as he gripped his cane and scooted back out the door.

The first people he saw when he got outside were the two gentlemen who had come to his office the day before. When they spotted Scrooge, they stopped in their tracks, not wishing another unpleasant meeting with the old miser.

But Scrooge simply slid down the staircase railing like a young schoolboy and shouted, "Merry Christmas to one and all!"

The two men took a step backward and exchanged wary glances.

"Good morning, gentlemen," Scrooge said, grinning with goodwill. "I've got something for you!"

Scrooge reached into his coat pocket, then grabbed the portly gentleman's hat and filled it with gold coins. Then he plopped the hat back on the man's head. With a befuddled look, the man took off his hat, and the coins rained down around him.

The other gentleman's jaw dropped open in amazement. "Twenty gold sovereigns!"

Scrooge barked out a laugh.

"Not enough?" he said. "Well, all right." And he stuffed the

first man's pockets with more gold coins.

"Fifty gold sovereigns!" cried Scrooge.

"Really, Mr. Scrooge," said the portly gentleman, "it's—"

"*Still* not enough?" cried Scrooge. And with that he tossed several bulging money bags at the two disbelieving men.

"You drive a hard bargain," Scrooge said. "Here you are— one hundred gold pieces, and not a penny more. Hee, hee!"

The two men were overwhelmed by Ebenezer Scrooge's generosity and couldn't thank him enough as they picked up the money. But Scrooge was already tripping gaily down the street, calling out "Merry Christmas!" to everyone he passed.

Scrooge was so giddy with happiness that he didn't watch where he was going, and before he knew it a horse-drawn carriage was almost upon him. The horse reared in front of him and came to a dead stop.

Scrooge looked up with a smile on his face and saw that the driver was none other than his nephew, Fred.

"Ah, Nephew," Scrooge shouted.

"Uncle Scrooge!" Fred answered with surprise.

"I'm looking forward to that wonderful meal of yours," Scrooge said.

"Well, I'll be doggoned," said Fred, smiling broadly. "You mean you're *coming*?"

"Of course I am," Scrooge cried, as if there had never been any doubt. "You know how much I like candied fruits with sugar cakes!"

Fred could only laugh in astonishment at his uncle's change of heart.

"I'll be over promptly at two," Scrooge said. And then he added with mock sternness, "Keep it piping hot."

"I will, Uncle Scrooge, I will," answered Fred. "And a very merry Christmas to you."

Scrooge waved Fred off with a chuckle and continued jauntily down the street. His top hat bobbed up and down on his head, keeping time with his steps.

Scrooge headed right for the poultry shop just a few doors away. There he bought a huge cooked turkey and all the trimmings for a bountiful holiday feast.

Next, he stopped at a charming little toy store tucked away in the middle of a busy street.

There were so many fabulous toys and games that Scrooge couldn't make up his mind what to buy. He solved his dilemma by telling the startled clerks to fill a bag with their very best wares.

A short while later Scrooge came out of the shop carrying a sackful of toys along with all the food.

"Keep the change!" he yelled back over his shoulder. "And now on to Cratchit's."

It didn't take Scrooge long to find Bob Cratchit's house. He remembered all too well where it was from his ghostly visit the night before.

He stood before the shabby dwelling and couldn't help giggling as he thought about what he was going to do. Just before he knocked on the door, he forced himself to put on a stern face.

Bob answered the door. When he saw his employer standing there, his mouth dropped open in surprise, but he recovered quickly. "Why, Mr. Scrooge," he said, "ah, Merry Christmas."

Scrooge barged in without waiting for an invitation. It was a perfect imitation of his old behavior.

"Merry Christmas, huh?" Scrooge growled, trying not to show his newfound happiness. "I've another bundle for you!"

"But, sir, it's Christmas Day," Bob exclaimed, casting a hopeless glance at his wife. Mrs. Cratchit and the children were huddled together at the other end of the room, anxiously watching Scrooge. All except Tiny Tim. He spied a teddy bear that was sticking out of the bag that Scrooge had brought with him. Now Tim was poking curiously at the bag behind Scrooge's back.

"Christmas Day, indeed," said Scrooge. "Christmas Day is just another excuse for being lazy!" he continued.

Scrooge was having a hard time keeping up this gruff manner. But he wanted his surprise to be all the more surprising when he sprang it. And so he went on:

"And another thing, Cratchit," he cried. "I've had enough of this half-day-off stuff. You leave me no alternative..."

Bob's face was getting paler by the minute, and his eyes looked as big and round as saucers. He was sure he was about to be fired.

"...no alternative," Scrooge went on, "but to give you—"

"TOYS!" piped Tiny Tim. He had opened the bag and was now pulling out one toy after the other.

"Yes—toys!" shouted Scrooge in glee.

Then he shook his head in good-natured dismay.

"No, no, no, no," Scrooge hastily corrected himself. "Not toys. I'm giving you a raise and making you my partner!"

"Your *partner?*" Bob asked in amazement.

"My partner," Scrooge repeated, laughing heartily. "And I can't think of a more deserving soul," he added.

By now Mrs. Cratchit and the other children had surrounded

the bag of gifts. When Mrs. Cratchit saw the big turkey and all the other good things to eat, her face lit up with joy. She took the turkey out and carried it to the table.

"Oh, thank you, Mr. Scrooge," said Bob.

Scrooge watched her for a moment, and then he turned to Tiny Tim and smiled. Tiny Tim smiled back and held out his arms. Scrooge felt a lump in his throat. It had been a very long time since anyone had shown him such a sign of affection and trust.

Scrooge picked up Tiny Tim, and as the little boy snuggled in his arms, Scrooge said, "Why I do believe that turkey weighs more than *you* do!

"Tsk, tsk, that will never do," continued Scrooge as he playfully pinched Tiny Tim's ribs. "We're going to have to fatten you up as quickly as we can. I will see to that personally!"

"We don't know how to thank you for all this," said Bob, spreading out his arms to encompass the food and gifts surrounding them.

"Stuff and nonsense!" said Scrooge. "It's Christmas!"

And with that, the other children laughed and went running up to Scrooge and Tiny Tim. Scrooge hugged each child and gathered them closer. Never in his life had he felt such joy.

"Merry Christmas, children," he said.

Then he turned to Bob and Mrs. Cratchit. "And a Merry Christmas to you both!" he said.

"Merry Christmas to us all!" cried Tiny Tim. "And God bless us, every one!"

Scrooge nodded. "Yes, indeed, God bless us, every one," Scrooge repeated as he basked in the warm glow that embraced him on that very merry Christmas Day.